THE HIGHWAY KIND

DEREK FLYNN

Copyright © 2024 Derek Flynn

All rights reserved.

ISBN: 9798320177519

"Usually I just walk these streets
And tell myself to care,
Sometimes I believe me,
And sometimes I don't hear."

- "The Highway Kind", Townes Van Zandt

CONTENTS

1 On Oakwood Street   5

2 The Last Chapter of Dreaming   13

3 Kingdom of the Mad   25

4 Deliver Us from Evil   37

5 Echo Park   53

6 The Artist   65

7 A Town Called Winter   79

8 Ghost Estate   89

FOREWARD

I love small towns.

Specifically, I love *American* small towns. Actually, I should qualify that as well. I love the kind of American small town that I imagined from the movies, books, and comics that I devoured as a teenager – having never set foot out of Ireland and imagining one stoplight towns shimmering in the desert heat. Movies like *Paris, Texas* and *The Last Picture Show*. Novels like *The Virgin Suicides* and *To Kill a Mockingbird*. And even now, decades later – having travelled all over the United States and realising that many of those small towns don't exist outside of fiction – I'm still fascinated by them.

I also love the music of these small towns – the songs of dead-end bars and motel rooms. So, I decided to take some of those songs as a jumping-off point for a collection of short stories. The title page of each story in this book has the name of the song that inspired it. There's also a link at the end of the book to a Soundcloud playlist featuring my versions of some of those songs.

The stories are not meant to reproduce or emulate the genius of the lyrics in these songs. Rather, they are sketches – snapshots of life – suggested and inspired by the songs. Some of the stories may even seem to have very little connection with the songs beyond what I can only call a feeling, or an emotion inspired by the song.

The title of the collection is also taken from a song – "The Highway Kind" by the great Townes Van Zandt. The highway kind may not always walk a highway. They may walk a boulevard in Paris, or the footpaths of a ghost estate in Ireland. But they are all linked by that same feeling.

I hope you enjoy your spin on the highway.

Derek Flynn, 2024

ON OAKWOOD STREET

("Tom Traubert's Blues" by Tom Waits)

ON OAKWOOD STREET

Ursula used to be an actress. Now, she's an alcoholic. She spends most of her days and nights in the same couple of bars on Oakwood Street, sitting in the corner by herself, drinking wine and writing poetry. She reads me one. It's good.

"I wrote that last night," she says. "Before I passed out."

She was a good actress, at least as she tells it. And she was on the up. She'd just landed a supporting role in a big Hollywood summer movie. The day she found out, she went out to lunch with some friends to celebrate. And one glass of wine turned into three, turned into five. By the time she got home that evening, she was hammered. As she got changed for bed, she tripped over a make-up case on the floor and fell – face-first – into a full-size mirror. The left side of her face hit the mirror; the glass smashed and carved a bloody furrow from her forehead to her chin. The doctors did the best they could to patch her up, but she was left with an inch-wide scar. She got some reconstructive surgery, but it was expensive. When the money ran out, she ended up back on Oakwood Street.

Funny thing about Ursula: she's obsessed with mirrors. She can't pass a mirror without staring at herself in it. Sometimes, she'll sit there for twenty, thirty minutes staring into it. We'll be in the bar and she'll go to the bathroom, and half an hour later, I'll have to go find her and she'll be sitting on the bathroom sink looking at herself in the mirror.

"Don't you ever just like looking at yourself?" she asks me one day.

"No. I tend to avoid mirrors."

"Why is that?"

"Because I don't like what I see."

Of course, she doesn't either. She's not staring at the good side of her face. She's staring at the scar. But she doesn't look sad. The whole time she's sitting there, she has a look of concentration, as if she's trying very hard to understand why something like that would happen. *A simple twist of fate*, as Dylan said. Something you can never understand.

I ask her what sounds like a stupid question – does she think she'd be happier if the accident had never happened, if she was still an actress in Hollywood? It comes out sounding like a cruel question, but I'm just curious. She looks at me through the end of an empty shot glass.

"Probably. I'd have money, maybe be married. Of course, I'd probably be a mindless drone, pinched and preened to within an inch of my life, spouting banal soundbites to Entertainment Tonight. But ... it seems to work for all those other actresses, right?"

When we have sex, she climbs on top and lets her long, black hair hang down over that side of her face. And when she sleeps, she turns her back to me, her face buried in the pillow. The only time she doesn't wear her hair down is when she's in the bars. Then, she ties her hair back, her scar on full show. It doesn't seem to matter then. Everyone in there has scars on their faces, real or not.

Because, with Ursula, I end up hanging out in the types of bars that I usually avoid. They're a far cry from the bars I play – and I'll play pretty much anywhere. These bars don't have music. There might be an old, dilapidated jukebox in the corner, but none of the barflies in there are interested in listening to it, or in wasting their last few cents on a tune. These bars are the last stop, the last exit. Pretty much every single person in there is cursed.

In the beginning with Ursula, I didn't notice it that much. She'd read me her poetry and talk about life; she was so intelligent and articulate that it's only when I began to see her in these bars – with these people around her – that I realised how far she'd fallen.

And that's when my worst instincts kick in. I want to say, *Look, why don't you just kick the sauce and clean yourself up? Get back on your feet*. But by saying that, I'm saying that their world is wrong.

Sure, she could opt out, just like people opt out of "normal" life. But most people don't opt out; most just choose to continue on, for better or worse. And that's what she was doing, that's what everybody else in the bar was doing. It doesn't make them bad, it doesn't make them good; it doesn't make them anything but human.

I watch the people in these places as they laugh and argue. They're no different to the people I play to every night. The only difference is the ones that I play to believe they have somewhere to go to when they leave the bar. But maybe they're the ones deluding themselves, believing that there's some point to it all, some point in trying to get somewhere, to get the job, the house, the car. Ursula and the rest of these people, maybe they're the ones who know the real truth.

And bars like this, they're everywhere. Just slightly out of view, down the end of some dark alley, or hidden ever so slightly behind the thin veil of normality. And you could walk into any of these places. You could sit down at the bar and order a beer. And you'd look around at the people there, talking, fighting, laughing. And one of them might even come up to talk to you. You might almost recognise him. He looks a bit like "The one most likely to" back in High School. But that couldn't possibly be this wretch standing in front of you.

And it might even be one of those nights – you stay, you get drunk, you fall around the bar, laughing and joking with them. But you get a sense of something, something not quite right. And when you leave the bar that night, that feeling stays with you. The same feeling you got before you plucked up the courage to walk in there in the first place. Because there was an aura about it you didn't like. The kind of place people would say, "Nah, I wouldn't go there." But you, you weren't like that. You were made of sterner stuff. But they were right. There *was* something. There was an air of despair in the place that was palpable. Something that clung to the people in there, clung to the walls. And now it was clinging to you to a certain degree. You wake the next morning, and you have a vague sense of something at the back of your mind, but, for some reason, you can't remember much. That's hardly surprising, you tell yourself, the amount of drinks you had. But something in the back of your mind will tell you –no, it's more than the drinks. It's something else. Some reason why you can't remember a single face, or a single name, or a single conversation that you had. And the next time you pass that bar, you won't go in. In fact, you might speed up a little as you pass the door. And you won't look in the window. Just in case somebody looks back.

THE LAST CHAPTER OF DREAMING
("Your Ghost" by Kirstin Hersh)

THE LAST CHAPTER OF DREAMING

Adrienne woke to the soothing voice of Sam Cooke. Turning over, she fumbled for the snooze button on the alarm clock, but thinking better of it, she turned it off instead and got out of the bed. It wouldn't do to be late three mornings in a row.

Downstairs she could hear John going through his usual morning routine. He was checking all the doors to make sure they were locked, which meant he had already polished his shoes, had his muesli and coffee, put on his holster and badge, and checked himself over in the hall mirror. She waited until she heard the front door close and his car pull out of the driveway before she went downstairs.

The kitchen, as ever, was immaculate. The cereal box had been put away and his bowl and cup were drying on the draining board. Every morning, as she surveyed the bastion of cleanliness, Adrienne was wracked with the desire to empty the contents of the cupboards out onto the floor. Of course, she never did. In a town like Thebes, Wyoming, they could commit you for less.

After taking a shower, getting dressed and skipping breakfast, she pulled her car out of the driveway. The drive into town along

Route 20 was as uneventful as ever: the usual steady stream of cars headed in the opposite direction for the textile factory. Sometimes, she swore to herself that the same cars passed, in the same order, every morning. She wondered how it was possible to live in such a sprawling, wide-open space, and yet feel so hemmed in.

It was 9.10 when she parked the car in front of The Runner Bean coffee shop. She could see Mabel glaring at her from inside.

"My God, Mabel, have you ever seen heat like this?" she said, bursting into the coffee shop. She walked past Mabel, and the customer she was serving, as fast as she could.

"You should get up earlier," Mabel said, her face obscured behind the steam from the coffee machine. "It's cooler."

Adrienne pretended not to have heard and closed the door of the broom closet behind her. Hanging up her coat, she heard the gurgle of the machine stop and Mabel's footsteps coming up to the door. Mabel's footsteps were unmistakable because, despite her age, (she claimed 48 although everyone knew it was closer to 58), she still retained the walk of her 21-year-old self.

Back in the annals of time, Mabel had been "Miss Thebes 1983"; an honour due, she claimed, to the twelve months of training she had received at the – now sadly defunct – "Thorpe School for Young Ladies". At this point in the story, Mabel would demonstrate the all-important walk, which had been drilled into them for twelve months.

This was an exact replica of the walk taking place outside the closet door. Adrienne heard her knock, and she opened the door slightly. Mabel's face appeared through the opening. She looked like a cartoon character, with her generously applied make-up, her enormous hair that doubled the size of her head, and the smell of cheap perfume that followed her like a wagon trail. Over Mabel's shoulder, Adrienne could see that the shop was empty.

"You know, Adrienne," Mabel began, with the perfect mix of fake concern and condescension. "You really need to try harder."

Adrienne squeezed past her. "Yeah, sorry. That morning rush must have wiped you out."

She went behind the counter and began to make herself an Americano. Seeing Mabel approach with her game face on, she decided against it. It would have to be an espresso. A very strong espresso. Mabel teetered ridiculously in her six-inch heels up to the counter.

"That's hardly the point, Adrienne. I have a business to run here. You can't just come wandering in every morning whenever you feel like it."

For what must have been the one-hundredth time, Adrienne asked herself why exactly it was she had taken this job. It wasn't like she needed the money; they would have been more than comfortable on John's salary. But John seemed to like the idea of his wife actually having a real job (as opposed to his mother, to whom work meant charity functions and manicures) and if she were to be honest, it was better than the alternative of dying the slow death of daytime soaps.

"You're right, Mabel. I'm sorry."

After they had closed for the day, Adrienne wasted as much time as possible cleaning up. She knew John would be late, as usual, and she didn't feel like another night alone in front of the TV.

She had locked up and was heading back to her car when she decided to take a walk down Main Street. Thebes was a typical, one-stoplight town. Its main street housed all it had to offer: if you didn't like what was contained there, you weren't going to like Thebes. At the end of Main Street, she stopped outside Clancy's. With its green, fluorescent shamrock, it was the faux-Irish pub that every main street in every town probably had (although she could never understand why the shamrock was always advertising American beer). She could hear the muted voices of the early starters and knew who they would be.

As she walked in, her suspicions were confirmed to the last one – from Wesley Reed, who had no doubt been propping up the bar since the early hours of the morning, to Sheri Mills, having her ritual evening dose of fortitude before going home to face her tyrant of a husband.

The bar itself, with its worn carpet and polyester wallpaper, looked like someone had installed a counter and some high stools in their living room. At the end of the room was a small space, loosely referred to as a dance floor, although the people who availed of it were usually the dregs of the bar, who – drunk and alone at 2am – joined forces for a few minutes of intimacy before facing home alone. Beside the dance floor, a dejected jukebox churned out yet another melancholy country song.

As she settled herself at the end of the bar, the bartender made his way down to her.

"Hi, Roy," she said.

"Hi, Ade. On your own tonight?"

It sounded more like an accusation than a question.

"Yeah ... John's working late."

"You gotta get him to ease up. We hardly ever see the Chief in here anymore. Except when he's pulling out drunks."

Roy flashed a smile that revealed a large gold tooth, the story of which he liked to recount endlessly on nights when he'd had too much tequila.

John had been Chief of Police for three years – long enough that most people in town simply referred to him as 'the Chief'. 'Say hi to the Chief for me,' they'd say, and Adrienne would feel like she was in a cop movie. But he had earned their respect. She wasn't sure if they liked him, but they respected him, and to John that was more important than anything else. That was why she knew how it would cut him up if he realised how much he'd lost hers.

"So, what can I do you for?"

"I think it's a tequila night, Roy."

He grabbed the bottle from the shelf and poured a shot.

"That bad, huh?" he said.

"Yup." She downed the shot and handed the glass back to him. "But it's starting to look better already."

Adrienne heard the door open behind her. Someone sat on the stool next to her and she looked round. He was a tall man – young, with dark hair and dark clothes. Roy made his way up the bar and the man ordered a whiskey.

"Another shot, Adrienne?" Roy asked.

"Yeah, thanks."

When Roy had walked away, the man turned to her.

"That's a beautiful name," he said.

She saw his face full on for the first time. At first glance he seemed young but looking at him now, it was hard to tell. There was a maturity there – hard to define, but it was there. In the dim light of the bar his eyes looked black.

"That's an unoriginal pick-up line," she said.

He took a drink from the glass and moved the whiskey around his mouth like a wine taster, savouring it, before swallowing.

"It means 'dark one'."

"Listen buddy, I'm married."

"Good for you. Did you know that?"

All the time he was speaking she kept looking at his eyes. It wasn't just a trick of the light – they were actually black. She had never seen someone with black eyes.

"Know what?" she asked.

"The meaning of your name."

"No. No I didn't."

"No one ever does anymore. Names used to be powerful. Nowadays, nobody cares."

She wasn't sure what he was talking about – the words were only half-registering. She didn't know if it was the tequila, but the more she stared at his eyes, the more disorientated she felt.

"What did you say it meant?"

"Dark one."

"Figures. So, what's yours?"

"Jal."

She half expected him to put out his hand as he said it, but he just kept looking at her.

"And what does that mean?"

"It means 'wanderer'." He said the word with what sounded like a sigh.

"And are you?"

"I am of no place and every place." He smiled again. She wasn't sure if she had heard him right.

"So, you're not from around here then?"

"Just passing through. I'm staying at the Safari Inn on Route 20." There seemed to be something in his eyes when he said it. "So, where's your husband?"

"What's that supposed to mean?" No sooner had she said it then she regretted how defensive it sounded.

"It's just a question."

"He's working." For the first time she pulled her gaze away from his eyes and back to her drink. "He's working and I'm here because if I have to spend another night alone watching crappy sitcoms, I'm liable to shoot myself." It was a relief just to say the words out loud, even though she couldn't believe that she'd done it.

"I'm sorry," she added.

"What for?"

"I don't usually make a habit of dumping my problems on complete strangers."

"Maybe you should."

She stared into his black eyes and for a second a moment of clarity hit her. She grabbed her coat and bag and almost fell off the stool in her haste to get to the door.

"I'm sorry," she said. "I have to go."

An hour later, she stood outside room 208 of the Safari Inn and knocked on the door. If anyone had asked her how she got there, she wasn't sure she could have answered. She was pretty sure she'd spent the past hour since she left the bar wandering the streets, but it was all a vague blur. They last thing she remembered clearly was the stranger's black eyes.

The man who had called himself Jal opened the door.

"Hello," he said. He didn't look very surprised. "Come in."

The room was dark, except for an odd candle here and there. There was a tray of leftover food on the table, and an empty wine bottle on the nightstand.

"The guy at reception told me your room number," Adrienne said, awkwardly.

He didn't answer. He was taking off her coat, his hand grazing her arm as he did so. He leaned into her, and she could feel his warm, wine-soaked breath on her cheek. She pulled back.

"What am I doing here?" she said.

"You tell me. You knocked on my door."

She felt the bed behind her and sat down. He walked over to the table and picked up a wine bottle.

"Would you like a drink?"

"No. Yes, yes, I need a drink."

He was standing over her with a glass of wine, which she took and almost downed in one gulp.

"Thanks," she said, coming up for air.

"So, where's your husband?" That question again.

"I'm leaving him." The words, when they came out, sounded like someone else was saying them.

"Why?" The bluntness of his question took her by surprise, and she looked at him as if she didn't understand.

"Why are you leaving your husband?"

"Because I don't love him. Because I haven't loved him for some time, and I don't know if he's ever loved me. I settled, I … what's that word … I acquiesced."

"And why did you do that?"

She got up off the bed and handed him the empty glass.

"Look, I better go. This is crazy."

"You're still worried what they'll say …"

"What?"

"You're terrified of making the wrong move, in case you'll become the one the town talks about next. What if you were seen? What would the ladies at the Rotary Club say? The police chief's wife in a hotel room with a strange man."

She felt like he was mocking her, and it hurt.

"You don't know me. You have no idea who I am."

"Don't I?"

"If you think I'm worried about tongues wagging, you're way off. What I'm worried about is what I'm doing here."

"It scares you?"

"Damn right, it scares me. Stuff like this doesn't happen to me."

"Because you don't let it. You *acquiesce* to the status quo. But you're not like them, Adrienne. That's why you're here. That's how you found me."

"Who are you?" The question sounded so obvious, she wondered why she hadn't asked it before.

"I'm the flipside. The reverse of the coin. I'm what you wanted to be when you were seventeen and dreaming about running away to the big city."

He was inches away from her, and although they weren't touching, it felt like his entire weight was bearing down on her. She wanted more than anything to just let go.

"I'm the thing you dream about every night ..."

She didn't pull him to her, and he didn't seem to move, yet somehow his face was buried in the cradle of her neck, his lips moving across her shoulder blades.

"Freedom," she thought she heard him say, but wasn't sure if it was her own voice she was hearing, and she remembered a poem she'd heard once about waking up from the last chapter of dreaming. The words resounded inside her head as his hands moved effortlessly up her body.

"Freedom," he said, and she knew it was his voice this time; she'd waited her whole life to hear it.

KINGDOM OF THE MAD
("Hope is a Dangerous Thing" by Lana Del Rey)

KINGDOM OF THE MAD

Someone once said that McLean looked more like a college campus than a psychiatric hospital. Sylvia thought they must have been nuts too. No matter how nice the view, a room with bars is still a prison.

Behind her, Anne was smoking, even though patients weren't supposed to smoke inside. Sylvia imagined that if the patients were told they could only smoke *inside*, Anne would have stood out in the rain. She frightened and fascinated Sylvia in equal measure.

Robert – their writing tutor – entered the room in a flurry of movement and wild hair.

"You can't smoke in here, Anne," he said.

Anne threw a disdainful glance in his direction. "They're not mine, they're Sylvia's."

"Anne!" Sylvia said.

"Oh, alright they're not Sylvia's, they're Dr Lazlo's."

Robert walked up to the desk at the top of the room and placed his books on it. "Dr Lazlo doesn't smoke," he said. His voice had the weary tone of a parent dealing with a precocious child.

"Oh, that's what he wants you to think, Bob," Anne said. "But I've seen him sneaking into the supply closet." She paused for effect. "Unless he's having an affair. You think that's what he's doing, Bob?"

Robert finally looked up at her over thick glasses perched halfway down his nose. "I'd prefer if you called me Robert."

"Why?"

"Because that's my name."

"But you look like a Bob. Don't you think so, Sylvia? Doesn't he look like a Bob?"

"What does a Bob look like?" Sylvia said.

"Like Robert."

Sylvia suppressed a laugh. Anne could also be funny. When she wasn't being terrifying.

Robert let out a sigh. "Can we dispense with the bon mots, Anne, and get down to work?"

Anne got up from her seat and walked, slowly and purposely, up to Robert's desk, as though she was putting on a show. Sylvia thought that perhaps Anne was always putting on a show. And when she moved, it was like one of those actresses from the movies, her hips moving rhythmically from side to side, her body wrapped tightly in a white dress like a mummy.

"What is it, Bob? Do free-spirited women scare you?" She took a drag from the cigarette and exhaled into his face. "Or is it just women in general? Your mother was a bit of a dragon, wasn't she?"

Robert didn't flinch. "There are a surprising number of things that scare me, Anne," he said, taking the cigarette from her mouth, "but I assure you, women aren't one of them." He stubbed the cigarette out on a piece of paper on the desk.

"Hey! That was my last cigarette."

"Good. Then maybe we can get to work."

Anne turned on her heels dramatically and stormed back to her seat. "Asshole," she muttered.

Sylvia looked up at Robert. "She doesn't mean that," she said, quietly.

Robert sat down behind his desk. "So ... what have you two been up to since last time?" he said.

"Oh, we've been living the high life," Anne replied. "Breakfast at Tiffany's ... a soiree at Marlon Brando's house." She paused. "Oh no ... wait, that's wrong. We've been taking meds and slowly dying from boredom. Yes. That's it."

"And how are you, Sylvia?" Robert said.

"I'm okay. I've been feeling a bit better this past week. Apart from last night."

"What happened last night?"

"I had a dream ..."

Anne looked over at her. "And?"

"I dreamt that all three of us were dead."

"Oooh." Anne was suddenly animated. "How did we die?"

"Anne," Robert said. "That's not really appropriate."

"Robert, death is our favourite subject."

"I died first," Sylvia went on. "I killed myself."

Anne jumped up from the chair and pointed a finger at Sylvia. "Thief! That was my death! You stole that from me!"

"Oh, stop it, Anne. You got there too in the end."

"Suicide?"

Sylvia nodded.

"How did I do it?"

"I don't know. Does it matter?"

"What about Robert? How did he die?"

"A heart attack. In the back of a taxi."

Anne sat back down. "Oh. That's good. I'm glad."

Robert leaned forward on the desk. "Sylvia, you know that's not real. It's only a dream." Sylvia could hear the concern in his voice.

"Of course," she said. "But it's fine. I got a new poem out of it."

"You wrote a new poem?"

"Yes ... but I don't know if it's any good."

"Oh, don't be so humble," Anne said. "You know Bob just *loves* your writing."

"I admire both of your work."

"Oh, I know you do, Robert, dear. But Sylvia's writing is so much more honest though, isn't it? I mean she really knows how to use all the crazy shit. Open the vein and bleed, like Hemingway said."

"It's not like that ..." Sylvia said, quietly.

"Sylvia, would you read me your poem?" Robert said. "I'd like to hear it."

Sylvia hung her head for a moment, nervously playing with a loose strand of hair. Then, in a quiet voice, she spoke about all of the times she'd tried to die. When she finished, she slid down into the desk a little further and didn't look up. There was silence in the room for a moment.

Then, Anne spoke: "You see, Robert, I told you she knows how to turn that shit into gold."

"Why do you have to be so mean?" Sylvia said, her head still hung.

"I'm not. I'm honestly not, Sylvia. I love it. You know how to get to the core and really mine that shit."

Robert turned to her. "Jesus Christ, Anne ... you try to turn depression and suffering into an artform. Mental illness is no different to you than pills or booze."

"Oh, they're *very* different. Bring nuts is far superior to any opiate."

"And you think that's a good thing? Do you really think Van Gogh *wanted* to be crazy? That he wouldn't have been happier out painting sunflowers all day instead of cutting off his fucking ear?"

"I think he couldn't have painted sunflowers *unless* he cut off his fucking ear. You're telling me it doesn't work for you, Robert? Using your pain for your art?"

Robert's expression changed. "That has no bearing on what we're doing here."

"Oh ... *it has no bearing*, does it not? Drop your New England affectations, Bob ... you're with the lunatics now. Why did you read us your poems then?"

"I thought it might help."

"Help us do what?"

"I don't know ... I ..."

"Stop it, Anne" Sylvia interrupted. "He can't write. He read us those poems because he's trying to write again."

"Yes ... and he's afraid to be honest."

Robert shook his head. "I don't know if I want to reveal that much of myself ..."

"No, Robert. You're afraid of upsetting your rich Mommy and Daddy and all those pilgrim ancestors of yours."

There was silence among the three of them. Finally, Sylvia spoke. "You know ... sometimes I think I'd be happy to just settle down with the husband, the house, the kids, the dog. Other times, I want to set fire to every fucking man on the planet."

"You've been hanging around Anne too long," Robert said.

"She's got the right idea."

"If men are so bad, Anne, why do you sleep with so many of them?"

"That's all they're good for. If it wasn't for that, they'd be extinct."

Sylvia stood up from her desk. "Ugh! It's impossible to have a conversation with you two," she said, walking towards the door.

"I'm sorry, Sylvia," Anne said. "Come back. Converse. Converse."

Sylvia stopped at the door and turned back. "Can we *please* talk about poetry?"

"Of course, we can, Sylvie."

"Oh, what does it all matter anyway?" Sylvia said. "I mean, really, what does it matter?"

"What do you mean?" Robert said.

Sylvia walked back over to her desk. "Well, we sit here talking about it every day ... but it makes no difference. It gets us all in the end anyway. It got Van Gogh ... it got us. It even got you, Robert."

Anne gave a sly grin. "Ooooh ... controversial."

"Sylvia, you know we don't talk about that here."

"Why not?"

"Yes, Robert," Anne said, "why not?"

"Because it's not helpful."

"Well, it could be helpful to us," Anne said. "After all ... you know all about the 'houses for the mentally ill'."

Robert flicked through the pages of the book in front of him. "I think it would be more productive if you read us your own words, Anne, instead of somebody else's."

"Oh really?" Anne said, standing up. "Well, here's one I prepared earlier."

Sylvia sat listening, as Anne talked about witches flying over houses at night and riding naked through villages.

"Anne, that's amazing," Sylvia said, when Anne had finished.

Robert nodded his head. "Yes … yes … very powerful."

Anne stared at him. "I'm not ashamed to die, Robert. Are you?"

"It's not about shame. I'd very much like to live on into grey and white hairs."

"Then say it! Say it for God's sake, man! Stop couching it in obscurity. 'Each of us holds a locked razor' … well, do you want to use it or don't you?"

"I do wish you'd stop regurgitating other people's words, Anne."

Anne walked up to the top of the room and stood inches away from Robert's face. Sylvia could see that he was growing uncomfortable.

"But they're not just somebody else's are they?" Anne said. "They're yours. Tell me, Robert … do you still hold a locked razor?"

"Anne, this isn't …"

"… appropriate. I know … you said. Well, damn your impropriety."

"Anne …" Sylvia said.

"Shut up, Sylvia. C'mon, Robert, tell us about the locked razor."

Robert dropped his head, avoiding her gaze. "Anne, please …"

"Tell us about all those thoroughbred mental cases they locked you up with."

"Stop it!" Robert shouted suddenly. "Stop it! My mind's not right!" His words echoed around the silent room as Anne and Sylvia stared at him.

"Excuse me … I have to …" The sentence hung unfinished in the air as Robert rushed out of the room.

Sylvia turned to Anne. "Should we go after him?"

"Honey, it's the loony bin, not a hotel bar," Anne said. "What do you think they're gonna do if you go running down the hall after him?"

They sat in silence until one of the orderlies entered.

"Mr. Lowell is not feeling well and had to go home," he said. "Both of you need to go back to your rooms now."

Sylvia looked at Anne. "Did we do that? Is that our fault?"

Anne didn't answer.

"Anne ..."

"No," Anne said, finally. "It's not our fault. It's like you said ... it gets us all in the end."

DELIVER US FROM EVIL
("My Father's House" by Bruce Springsteen)

DELIVER US FROM EVIL

I'm not sure if I ever saw my father actually cry but I'm pretty sure the closest he ever came was the day I made my first communion.

My father was a stock Irish-Catholic – stoic and obedient. He never talked about religion much, but he turned up to mass not only on Sundays but, if he could, a couple of times a week as well. And then there was the religious paraphernalia that populated the house. I remember him standing at the mirror getting dressed, the stark crucifix suspended against his white vest; the Sacred Heart picture that hung in the dining room with its Catholic fetish of blood and suffering; the rosary beads dangling from the car rear-view mirror and the little statue of St. Martin on the dashboard. They weren't oppressive things in a child's life – if anything, I simply remember them as commonplace, like family portraits or ornaments – but they instilled this idea of my father as a man whose faith was a part of who he was. Take it away and he wouldn't have been the same man.

And so, when I turned seven and marched up the church to taste the tiny wafer that they told me was the body of Jesus, my father stood in the back, a grin from ear to ear and a moistness in his eyes that he would have no doubt laughed off if anyone had noticed.

They say the Catholic Church is a lot like the mafia – you never really get out. And I suppose I've always had a weird fascination with the rituals of the church. In religion class all that year, we were taught about transubstantiation and how we would be eating the body of Jesus, but no matter how many times they said it, I don't think I ever really got it. I think I understood it as a metaphor – even though I was only seven – but these guys didn't deal in metaphors: to them it was the real thing.

So, as I walked up that church, my new communion suit itching all over and my rosette pinned to my chest, I observed the whole thing with some bemusement. Even when the priest handed me the communion wafer and whispered, "Body of Christ", I was fascinated not only by the ritual itself but by their *belief* in the ritual. And, indeed, my father's belief.

It was a few weeks after my communion that I saw my first dead body. My paternal grandfather had died, and we were going back to Ireland for the funeral. I had been born in America, so I never knew any of my grandparents, except for the cards that came at Christmas and on my birthday, the dollar bills falling from them like snow.

I remember how excited I was at the time – my first time on a plane, my first trip abroad. My first trip *anywhere*. So, while the adults were grieving, I was already planning my holiday.

We touched down in Shannon Airport at six in the morning and it was the coldest, greyest day I'd ever seen. I often heard my mother bemoan the Irish weather but never really imagined it was as bad as she said. It was. As we walked out the doors of the airport, a wet mist descended on us that didn't lift for another five days.

But truth be told, I didn't care.

We were met at the airport by my father's brother, who looked like my father dressed as a farmer. I remember thinking how awkward they looked together. My uncle seemed taken aback when my father went to shake his hand. My mother said how sorry she was, and he just nodded.

She did most of the talking in the car on the way down as my father gazed out the window at the passing fields. I couldn't tell if it was nostalgia or relief he was feeling.

It didn't take long to figure out what my mother was feeling, however. Within a couple of days, she was already talking about moving home. I was staying with her in my grandparent's house, while my father stayed in the family home with his brother and mother. All day long the doorbell rang as old friends and other members of the family came by to see how she was and get all the gossip about living in America. And she wasn't shy about letting them know just what she thought of life in America. *You should come home*, they told her, and my mother would nod. "But he'll never leave," she'd say, quietly, under her breath. My grandmother would be watching her closely.

"A woman's place is with her husband," she'd say, and my mother and her friends would fall silent.

The second night there, the wake was held in the family home. I remember the argument my parents had that day about whether or not I should go. My mother was shouting at my father, saying I was too young to be exposed to something like that, and he was shouting back that I'd made my communion and that meant I was old enough to pay my respects like any good Catholic.

"I'm going to walk into that house and my son's going to walk in with me," he said.

Later, I often wondered if my father was simply using me as a trophy, something to show off. *Look at my boy, all grown up.* Or maybe just doing it to get at my mother. But at the time, I just felt happy – wanted.

And my father won. I turned up in my communion suit, with my solemn but proud-looking father and my mother who looked even more unhappy than the other people at the wake.

When we entered the house, it was like stepping back in time. The walls were whitewashed, the ceiling low, and a fire blazed in the corner of the room, the smell of peat smoke mixing with the smell of tobacco and whiskey. I saw my father's mother for the first time. She looked like something from the Middle Ages with her shrunken, wrinkled face underneath the black shawl. Despite this, everyone seemed to be chatting and drinking and eating. It looked like a grown-up's party, albeit a quieter one than I was used to. I was offered a soft drink and asked if I would like something to eat. They even told me that there were other kids out back. I had no idea why my parents were so sad about going to wakes. Until my father led me into another, darker room. And there it was.

On the other side of the room – underneath a framed picture of the Pope – was a coffin. An open coffin.

And inside lay my grandfather, dressed in his best Sunday suit, with a glass of whiskey at his head. I wasn't sure if he was dead or just sleeping, like in the vampire movies, but either way I knew I didn't like it much. My mother took my hand, gave it a squeeze, and flashed a reassuring smile. My father leaned down closer to me.

"Michael, this is your Grandad, Stephen. He got sick and passed away. We're going to say some prayers for him so he can go to heaven."

I nodded and followed them to the side of the coffin where the three of us knelt, clasped our hands, and bowed our heads. I felt it then as I knelt there, my parents by my side, the distant clatter of voices like dishes. I felt the pull of the body that lay in the coffin, a macabre fascination with death, with wanting to know the story behind the cold, grey face.

This is not it, the voice seemed to say to me, *this is not death. Death was what I looked like before this.* Years later, I read about a poet who said he could see 'the skull beneath the skin'. That was what the body seemed to be telling me – about 'the skull beneath the skin'.

There were a number of other people kneeling around the bed and my father was reciting the rosary. Two of the men were priests. I don't remember much about them now, apart from the way everyone fussed around them. I'd seen priests in America, but they were never treated anything like these two men. Everything anyone said to them was prefaced with a "Yes, Father" or "No, Father". Women clucked around them. Even my father seemed more soft-spoken than I'd ever heard him when he was with them.

I remember thinking that being a priest didn't seem like such a bad vocation.

The week came to an end too soon and we were due to leave the next morning. My mother was supposed to be packing but all I could hear coming out of her room was what sounded like her crying and my grandmother shouting at her. Eventually, my grandmother walked out, slamming the door behind her. She came down the stairs like a bull, charging past me where I was lying on the floor playing with a toy, and went out to my grandfather in the kitchen.

"You better go up and talk some sense into that daughter of yours," I heard her shout. My grandfather came to the door of the kitchen, glanced over at me, gave me a wink, and closed the door. I couldn't hear anymore. A little while later, my grandfather came out of the kitchen and went upstairs. My grandmother followed and packed me off to bed. As I lay in the small box room, looking at the shadows on the ceiling, I could still hear my mother crying.

The next morning, my father's voice woke me up at six o' clock.

"C'mon, Michael. We've got a plane to catch."

I got up, threw my dressing gown on and followed him out onto the landing. He was knocking on the door of my mother's room.

"Sheila, you ready?" he said. "We have to go."

My mother came out onto the landing and glanced over at me standing at the bedroom door.

"Michael, go back into your room," she said.

My father was staring at her.

"Why aren't you dressed?"

I went back into the room but left the door ajar.

"I ... I'm staying on here a while. Me and Michael."

She could barely get the words out, her voice was shaking so much. I couldn't see my father's face, but I could imagine his expression.

"What the hell are you talking about?" he said.

"I can't go back there yet. I miss my family, my ..."

"I am not even going to discuss this! Get into that room and get your stuff together. We're already late as it is."

My mother didn't answer but she also didn't move. I heard someone come up the stairs. It was my grandfather's voice.

"Sheila, you should do as Declan says. You don't want to miss your plane."

"I don't want to go, Daddy. I told you that last night."

"I am not going to discuss this in front of the whole world, Sheila," my father said. "Get your things. The car is waiting."

He came into my room and told me to get dressed. I did so, all the while listening to the voices on the landing getting more and more animated. Once I was dressed, I walked out of the room. My father took my hand and started to lead me down the stairs.

"What are you doing?" my mother said.

"You want to stay, stay. But don't think I'll be leaving him here with you."

"Declan, you leave that child alone," she shouted, running down the stairs after him.

My father ignored her and kept going. When we got to the bottom, my mother grabbed him by the arm. He let go of my hand and swung around to face her so fast, I thought he was going to hit her. He grabbed her and pushed her up against the wall. I'd never seen him raise a hand to her before. There was fear in her expression, and a hostility in his voice that had only ever been hinted at.

"This is how it's going to happen," he said. "I'm taking Michael to the car and I'm going to wait for ten minutes. If you're not out there by then, we're leaving. You will never see either of us again. As far as I'm concerned you can rot here."

He continued to stare at her for a few moments in silence, as if to drive his point home. The he took my hand and walked out to the car. I could hear my mother sobbing behind me. I sat in the car, staring at the clock on the dashboard, a sick heaving in my stomach. Eight minutes later, my mother walked out the door, her suitcase in her hand. My grandfather called out to her to say goodbye, but she didn't turn around.

She didn't speak another word the whole way back.

As time went on, the dead body I'd seen at the wake came to haunt me more and more. And it wasn't just the dead body: it was what my father had said about the prayers and the soul trying to make its way to heaven. Why did they need those prayers to get to heaven? Didn't everyone just go to heaven anyway, as long as they'd been a good person? So, hadn't Granddad Stephen been a good person? My fascination with this started to turn into an obsession.

Every Sunday after mass there would be the Sunday roast. This was an extravagant affair that took place in alternating houses, but with the same cast of characters. It usually involved at least three or four families squeezed around the dining table and various other fold-out tables and chairs. The itinerary for the Sunday was always the same. My parents and I would go to the local Catholic Church, where a handful of other churchgoers – mostly Mexican and Spanish – went. I think it always annoyed my parents that they were stuck in with the immigrants, while all their other friends were across town at their churches. But, at that time, living in Grey River, Wyoming, meant St. Mary's Church or conversion. After my father died, my mother stopped going to mass. I don't know if it was because it was just her and the Mexicans left, or because she just stopped believing.

After mass, we'd head home, and slowly the other families would start arriving one by one, laden down with plates of food. My mother would tell them they shouldn't have but would snatch it off them just as quick. I'd go play with the other kids out back; the boys playing soldiers, the girls playing house.

Inside, the work would begin, with the women immediately heading for the kitchen, and the men heading first to the fridge for beer, and then, to the couch and TV. After a glorious spread, the women would once again retreat to the kitchen to clean up, while the men would once again assault the fridge and then the couch, or if it was a summer's day, the porch.

It was on one of those warm days a few weeks after the wake that I asked my father about the prayers.

"Why do the dead people need the prayers?" I asked him.

"Because of purgatory," he said.

I knew I'd heard the word before, but I wasn't really sure what it meant.

"Don't they teach you about purgatory in religion class?" my father said.

I shook my head.

"Typical," he said. "Ever since Vatican II, they've done away with everything. When a person is dying, a priest has to come and give them a final blessing called last rites. That means that all their sins are taken away and they can go straight to heaven. But if a person dies before the priest comes, then they haven't been forgiven and they have to go to purgatory."

"Is that like hell?"

"Sort of, but not as bad. But the good thing about purgatory is that all the souls who go there can get out and go to heaven if enough people on Earth say prayers for them. That's why we said prayers for Grandad Stephen."

After the dishes had been washed up and the game had finished, all the adults would sit around together – if it was summertime, out in the back, or else in what my parents called the 'sitting room'.

It was at those times that I'd notice how differently my parents acted with each other. For just that brief moment in time, they'd look happy. Gone was the tension and the antagonism. They would laugh, maybe even share a joke. That was one of the few times I would see them actually smile at each other. Maybe it was the company. Later, when everyone was gone, they'd clean up the mess in silence and go to bed. Or, if they were in someone else's house, they'd drive home in silence, unless my mother turned on the radio. After which, my father would turn the volume down slightly.

It took me a long time to realise that this was just how my parents were. This was the life they'd chosen for themselves and that – to them – wasn't necessarily a bad thing. It just was.

The fact of the matter was – despite the couple of major bust-ups I'd been witness to – they actually rarely argued at all. Most of the time they were just … I suppose the word is 'tolerant' of each other. My father went out and worked and brought the money home and paid the bills, and never complained; my mother cooked and cleaned and did everything else that was to be done without complaining either. Yet, neither seemed particularly happy with their lives. Obviously, for my mother, it was because he'd dragged her to the other side of the world. But, after her initial act of defiance, she simply set about making a life for herself and never said much more about it. It was almost as if she'd taken my grandmother's words to heart.

My father was a little harder to figure out. He'd pretty much gotten what he wanted in life, but he still didn't seem particularly happy with it. He'd laugh with his workmates, and occasionally share a joke with my mother, but most of the time he was his strict, sombre self.

I asked my mother about it one day.

"Mom, why is Daddy not happy?"

"What makes you think he's not happy?"

"He doesn't smile much. Or laugh."

"That doesn't mean he's not happy, Michael. That's just his way."

And the fact was, she was right. He wasn't a cruel man or an evil man; that was just his way. He was a man of few words, a strict man, and a man of steadfast morals, but he wasn't some kind of ogre. I suppose, it would have made things easier for me if he was. If I could say that he beat me every night and starved me into submission, but it wasn't like that at all. He raised his voice to me plenty of times, but rarely his hand. That wasn't his way. His way of getting to you was psychological. He'd continually push me, needle me, always trying to get me to go that bit further, even if I wasn't capable of going. Maybe that's why it stayed with me all my life. Because that kind of pressure gets under your skin and you never shake it. It was only later, looking back, that I realised that that was how he was raised. He didn't know any better. It was just his way.

My father's explanation about purgatory fed my fascination with dead bodies. I'd stopped focusing on my dead grandfather and had moved onto the dead in general. Having heard my father's explanation, my imagination ran wild. I imagined what purgatory looked like and what the people did there while they were waiting for the prayers that would release them.

I plagued my father with questions but after the initial information he'd given, he seemed to have little to add. I then moved onto the priest who taught me religion after school at St. Mary's, but he didn't seem too keen to want to talk about it.

I went to after-school classes at St. Mary's because, much to my father's consternation, there was no religion taught in the public schools. Most of the schools in Ireland, my father would tell me, were run by priests or brothers, and you got a proper religious education. Not like the heathens in the public school system. To be honest, I don't know if my father thought that the after-school classes were much better. They were run by an Irish priest as well, but there, any similarities seemed to end. He was young – thinking back, he looked like little more than a kid himself. I presume he was fresh out of the seminary and had been handed this backwater church that no one else wanted. But he took it, and he taught us kids with great enthusiasm. I didn't realise it back then, but looking back now, I can see how progressive an attitude he had. Maybe, he was part of a new generation, moving away from the dark, repressive days of the Catholic Church. I don't really know, but I do know he was an antidote to my father's fire and brimstone.

I stayed back one day after class and asked him about purgatory. He seemed to squirm a bit in his seat when I said the word.

"Well, the church today tends to focus on some of the more positive aspects of Jesus' love."

I didn't know what that meant.

"But, when you die, do you still go to purgatory?" I asked him.

"You go to heaven, Michael."

"But what if you've sinned? Don't you have to repent before you die?"

"Well, you repent your sins every time you go to confession. If you lead a good life, and confess your sins regularly, there's no reason why, when you die, you shouldn't go to heaven."

"But what if I die before I make my confession?"

He smiled to himself.

"Michael, none of the sins you could commit are the kind of sins that could keep you out of heaven. The important thing to focus on is Jesus' love. Jesus promised us all a place in heaven because he loves us. He loves us so much that he gave up his own life to take on our sins, so that we would be able to find a place in heaven."

I didn't think my father would be too happy with that explanation. It didn't sound like there was quite enough suffering in it.

A few nights before I made my first communion, my father sat me down on the couch and told me about when he had made his communion. I've never been able to remember anything else he told me save for one thing. He said that they were told by the priests that if they didn't make their Holy Communion, then the devil would come to them in the middle of the night and burn them alive in their beds. After he finished telling me the story, we both sat in silence. I waited for him to say that it was just a scary story that the priests made up. But he said nothing more; he just sat there staring into the fire.

ECHO PARK

("Carmelita" by Warren Zevon)

ECHO PARK

When Angie got home, the house was in darkness. She made her way from the hall to the living room, turning on the lights as she went. She found Jimmy sitting in a chair bathed in the glow of the TV.

"Hey, babe," she said.

"Hey." He didn't look up.

"How was your day?"

The question was redundant because she knew the answer. Most of his day had been spent in the position he was in right now. But as soon as she had the thought, she regretted it. She didn't want to be *that* kind of girlfriend. Because Jimmy wasn't *that* kind of boyfriend. She knew he was trying hard to find work. The problem was work didn't want to be found.

"You hungry?" she said. "I was gonna order some takeout."

"Sure."

"What would you like?"

Jimmy leaned his head back, closing his eyes. "I don't care. Whatever you're having."

Angie walked over and sat on the arm of the chair.

"So ... *my* day was fine," she said.

"Yeah?"

She waited for him to say something more but there was nothing.

"Wesley wants me to do more shifts at the restaurant."

Jimmy opened his eyes and looked up at her. "Well, that's good, right?" He suddenly seemed interested in the conversation.

"They're the worst shifts. Nothing but weirdos and handsy truck drivers."

"But that's what you want, right?"

"What?"

"Well, that's what you wanted … more money. I mean, that's why you were doing … the other thing."

And there it was, she thought.

"Is *that* what this is about?"

He looked at her blankly. "What *what* is about?"

"This permanent mood you've been in lately?"

"I'm not in a mood."

Angie got up from the arm of the chair and headed out to the kitchen. "Can't we get past this?" she called back to him. She rifled in the kitchen drawer for the Chinese takeout menu even though she already knew what she was going to have. Jimmy appeared in the kitchen doorway.

"And how am I supposed to do that?" he said.

"It's just a job, Jimmy."

"Really? Is it though?"

"You said you were okay with this. It's been a month."

"Yeah, a whole month I've been going around with an image of you naked on a bed and a guy standing over you with a fucking whip." For the first time, his voice had risen above a whisper.

"Jesus, Jimmy … how many times are we gonna replay this? I told you … you should have called ahead."

"Oh, so it's *my* fault? You don't think maybe you should have given me a heads up that you were doing God-knows-what with some pervert …"

"They're not perverts. Some people just have different tastes."

"Different tastes is Coke or Pepsi, Angie."

"Jesus, I never knew you were such a square."

She slammed the takeout menu down on the kitchen counter and pretended to look through it. Jimmy walked up to her.

"Oh, *I'm* a square because I don't want guys tying you up and beating the crap out of you?"

"You know they don't do that. I don't let them do anything I don't want them to do. They're very respectful."

"Aw, isn't that nice?"

"How long are you gonna keep on about this?"

"I don't know. How long are you going to keep doing it?"

"I already told you, it's how I make my money."

"Lots of people need money, Angie. They find ways of making it that doesn't involve … that." He paused. "Besides, that's not all that's bothering me."

For a second, Angie considered just walking out the door and stopping the conversation dead in its tracks. But she knew it would still just be waiting for her when she got home again.

"Go on," she said.

"You said … you said you like it … what they do to you …"

"I said I liked *it*. I didn't say I liked *them* doing it to me."

"What's that supposed to mean?"

She felt like she was explaining something to a three-year-old, but she did her best to keep any condescension out of her voice. "It means ... I like it when I do it with someone I care about. With them, it's just a job." She paused for a second and then looked at him. "I told you ... you could do it if you like."

"That's not what you said ..."

"What I meant was, I wasn't doing anything that I didn't want to do. They don't hurt me. But they also don't ... y'know ... they don't *do* anything for me."

"I don't really see how that makes a difference."

"How can you not? If you did it, I'd enjoy it. When they do it, it doesn't bother me ... it doesn't hurt me ... but it also doesn't do anything for me. It's just a job."

"That's like saying being a hooker is just a job."

The word felt like a slap in the face.

"I'm not a fucking hooker!"

She pushed him out of the way hard and noticed him grimace as he hit his hip off the counter edge.

"I know that ..." he called after her. "I'm just saying ..."

She stopped in the doorway and turned around. She could feel the blood rushing to her face and the words tumbling from her mouth.

"Well, don't just say, okay? How dare you get all fucking sanctimonious on me. You don't know me. You blew in here ... you could blow out just as quick. I have to live."

"I know, but ..."

"I don't fuck them. I'm not a prostitute. It's something they like to do, something I don't mind them doing, and something I like getting paid for. You think I'd be living in this house on waitress tips?"

She walked out of the kitchen and back into the living room, looking for her bag. As she scanned the room for it, she sensed him walk up behind her.

"I'm sorry ... I didn't mean that ..."

"Where the fuck is my bag?"

He pointed to the floor where she'd dropped it when she came in. She picked it up and rooted around inside for her phone.

"Did you ever cheat on someone?" she said, as she took the phone out of her bag.

"What?"

"Did you? Honestly?"

He thought about it for a second, and then said, "Yeah."

"Right. So, don't you think that's worse? I'm not cheating on you. I'm not having sex with anyone else." She was looking straight at him, but he avoided her gaze, staring instead at the floor. "What? You're not gonna talk to me now?"

"I don't know what else to say." His voice was quiet again.

"Jesus ... fine. If it bothers you that much, I won't do it anymore, okay? I'll find some other way to make money. I'll take all the shitty shifts at the diner, if that'll make you happy."

She tossed the takeout menu she was still holding onto the couch and headed for the front door.

"Where are you going?" he called after her.

"Out. Order your own fucking dinner."

***

As Jimmy closed the front door behind him, he could hear Angie's voice from upstairs.

"Oh, 'TankMan'. You're very kind. I do try to keep myself in shape. I work out whenever I can."

Jimmy stopped at the bottom of the stairs and listened.

"Hi, 'Traderblue'. It's good to see you again. I hope you're feeling better. Hahaha, well, you know you gotta help me hit my target before the thong can come off. So hit me up with some credits, bad boy."

Jimmy walked into the kitchen, grabbed himself a beer, and went back into the living room. As he sat down on the couch, he heard Angie say, "Okay, guys, I'm afraid I gotta go. I know, I know. But I'll be back tomorrow. Thanks so much for hanging out with me. Bye bye, guys."

Jimmy drank his beer in silence, staring at the black screen of the TV. He heard Angie come down the stairs.

"Hey babe," she called in from the hall. "I didn't know you were home. I'm grabbing a beer. You want one?"

"I'm fine."

Angie came in from the kitchen with a beer and sat down on the couch next to Jimmy.

"I'm shot," she said, taking a slug of beer.

"Must be tiring all right, laughing it up with your pals."

Angie looked at him. "What's wrong with you?"

Jimmy moved so suddenly that he almost spilled his beer.

"What's *wrong* with me? Oh, I dunno. I'm just sitting here like some dumb idiot while my girlfriend is upstairs flashing her tits at random strangers."

"Oh, not this again."

"Yes, *this* again. I mean ... what does that make *me*, Angie? All these guys looking at you naked ... you laughing and joking with them ... what's left for me? That's why you go out with someone, right? Because there's a part of them that only you get to see. So, what's the point if every other guy gets to have what I have."

Angie got up from the couch and started to walk out of the room.

"You're such a fucking idiot."

"Oh, so you're just gonna walk away from me now?"

"Yes, I'm gonna walk away, because I'm not having this pointless, stupid fucking argument for the hundredth time."

Jimmy got up from the couch and followed her out into the kitchen. Angie was opening the back door.

"Are you telling me I'm not right?" Jimmy said.

Angie stood out on the back step and took a packet of cigarettes from her pocket.

"Yes, I'm telling you you're not right. I'm telling you you're fucking stupid. You get the real me, not the made-up shit that I do to earn some money."

"You said you were just stripping ... but it's more than that. You're talking to them."

"That's how I make *more* money."

"It's like you're cheating on me."

"Oh, for fucks sake!" Angie took a cigarette from the pack and lit it. "You wanted me to stop the sub/dom stuff, so I stopped. Now you want me to quit this as well? And how are we gonna pay the rent on this place with my shitty tips and your minimum wage?"

"We'll get by."

"Get by? I don't wanna get by. I don't want to be those people, Jimmy. I want to have a nice apartment ... I want to go out to dinner ... I want to go on vacation."

She took a drag from the cigarette, inhaling and exhaling the smoke in an angry, fluid movement, all the while holding his stare.

"And you're happy to pay for it by doing this?" he said.

"Yes ... yes, I am. And I've had enough of you slut-shaming me."

"What does that mean?"

"It means I'm sick of you trying to tell me what I can do with my body. And trying to make me feel ashamed."

"I'm not trying to make you feel ashamed. I'm just telling you how I feel."

"Well, guess what? You don't get to tell me that. I *am* with you ... no one else. If you can't see that, then maybe we shouldn't be together at all."

She tossed the cigarette to the ground, crushing it with her heel and walking back inside. "What is it that bothers you?" she went on, as she closed the back door again. "That your girlfriend flashes her tits at some strangers on the internet, or what people would think if they knew?"

"Maybe it's both."

"Who cares? Who gives a fuck what people think? I mean, what does it matter at the end of the day? We all go around freaking ourselves out about what people will think about us ... and then you realise ... everyone is doing the same thing. We all think the world revolves around us. It's like the world is a movie, and we all think we're the main characters. But what if we're not? What if we're just secondary characters? What if we're just supporting roles? Extras?"

Jimmy was silent for a moment, his expression blank. "What the fuck are you on about?"

Angie was about to say something else, but instead she just said, "Nothing. I have to go to the diner."

After she had gone, Jimmy got another beer and sat back down on the couch, scrolling through his phone. He typed something in and continued scrolling. Eventually, he stopped scrolling and pressed play on a video. As the sounds of a couple having sex started, Jimmy glanced around him, watched the video for a moment, and then unzipped his pants.

THE ARTIST

("Simple Twist of Fate" by Bob Dylan)

THE ARTIST

I was an artist once. A damn good one too. I lived in Paris. Of course. Where else? All my life growing up, that's all I ever wanted to be: an artist. From the moment I picked up a crayon as a kid, that's all I ever did. Draw people. I was fascinated by everything about them. When I was younger, I'd just draw their faces. Faces, endlessly. I got so good at it, when I went to art school, they told me I was gifted. I got a scholarship to go and paint in Paris for a year. Montparnasse. I was out for glamour and adventure. I was going to be Picasso. You know, without all the asshole stuff.

I became fascinated with the human figure. Still am. I don't draw anymore but I was always fascinated with the body. It's the most amazing thing. Skin, skin tones, the texture of skin. There's nothing like the human form, man or woman.

There was a guy lived in my doorway in Paris. It was a vestibule, and at night, if it was cold or raining, he'd sleep there. At first, he always took off before I got up. I knew he was there because I'd come home late a few nights and seen him. If he saw me coming, he'd scurry out of the doorway and sit out on the street. Initially, I was a little weirded out by it. I'd seen it happen in other places, so I knew it wasn't just me, but still ... the idea of some homeless guy living in front of my house made me a little uneasy. I mean, I'll admit it, I was prejudiced. I saw homeless guy, I thought, dirty, alcoholic, maybe even dangerous.

One morning I got up early and he was still there. He started to scramble away when I opened the door, but I stopped him. "You don't have to," I said. "It's okay."

He looked at me with these lost ... I was about to say 'dead' eyes, but they were far from dead. But they *were* lost. He stood up and faced me. He was deceptively tall. I'd only ever seen him lying on the ground. Tall and wire thin. Do you know the artist Egon Schiele? He did these figures, they're painfully angular. Their faces, as well as their bodies. He used to do self-portraits of himself. They're astonishing. Long, thin fingers ... wirey arms. Bones protruding everywhere. Cheekbones, shoulder blades. Just bone and hair. That's exactly what he looked like. I remember thinking that the very first moment I saw him up close. I mean he was just wearing a ragged old t-shirt. He had a blanket wrapped around him, but he dropped it when he stood up and I could see his frame. Obviously, he hadn't eaten in a long time. The first thing I thought was, I want to draw him. I don't think I actually thought about being attracted to him or anything like that. It was just purely aesthetic, initially.

He didn't speak to me that first day, so I let it go. I thought he was probably shy, maybe embarrassed, having to sleep in my doorway. But I got up early the next few mornings, and I passed a few words with him. He spoke back. Just small talk. Then, one morning, I told him I was going to the creperie around the corner and asked him if he'd like something. He said no. I figured he would. But I continued to get up every morning and ask him. It wasn't like me, getting up at that hour. I was never a morning person. I used to like to paint all through the night, sleep in until noon. But I'd suddenly lost interest in painting anything else – I just wanted to paint him. So, I started going to bed earlier and getting up earlier. I knew he'd need to trust me before I could ask him to pose for me. I needed to make a connection with him and to do that I'd have to speak to him every morning. I spent two weeks going to the creperie every morning and asking him if he wanted anything. Eventually, one morning, I said, "Look, I understand you don't want to take a coffee from me, but really, it's just a cup of coffee. I'd feel better if you would take it. And maybe even something to eat." He shrugged and said, "Okay." It got easier after that.

He started to look a little bit better. It was just coffee and a croissant, but it seemed to nourish him to some degree. I wished I could have done more but all during the day I never saw him. Or in the evening. Never until night. It got to the stage where I couldn't go to bed until I heard him outside. I'd sit in the hallway, just inside the door, right around the time I knew he was going to come. I'd hear his footsteps, I'd hear him lie down on the step, and pull his blanket around him. Then I could sleep.

One day, I plucked up the courage to ask him.

"Why don't you come for something to eat tonight?"

"No. Thank you, but I couldn't."

"Please," I said. "I'm cooking for myself. It's no fun. I like to cook. And I'd like to have someone to cook for." It made me sound lonelier than I thought I was, to be honest. He must have felt sorry for me because he said yes.

When he arrived that night, I asked him if he wanted to take a shower. He looked offended.

"Oh, come on," I said, a little impatiently. "You've been sleeping on my doorstep for the past two months. In the same clothes. I know you haven't showered. Why don't you just take the opportunity."

"I shower every day in a hostel."

"Oh," I said. "I'm sorry. Your clothes, then. I could wash them for you. I have some men's clothes. In my studio. The models sometimes wear them. You could put those on. I'll get yours back to you once they're dry."

He nodded and followed me into the studio. I pointed to a pile of old clothes in the corner.

"Take your pick," I said. "There must be something there that fits. I'll leave you get changed. I'll be out in the kitchen."

When he came out of the studio, he looked even more gaunt. The clothes were too big for him. He shuffled uneasily over to the table. I handed him a plate of pasta, and he dug into it without saying a word. He cleaned the plate in minutes.

"Would you like some more?"

"I shouldn't make a pig of myself," he said.

"Please. It's a compliment." It wasn't, not really. At that stage, I figured he'd be as content eating pigswill.

We talked through dinner. Or rather, I talked, he ate. He added in a few occasional words, but all just small talk. I told him all about myself, where I was from in America, what I was doing in Paris, the things I loved about the city. He nodded and agreed and told me of other places that I didn't know about but told me nothing about himself.

"Where in America are you from?" I asked him.

"Nowhere you'd know."

"Small town?"

"Doesn't even qualify as a town." He must have seen some slight exasperation in my face because he went on. "In Minnesota."

"I've never been to Minnesota."

"Don't bother."

"What about you?"

"What?"

"Have you travelled much? I mean apart from here, obviously."

"This was my first time out of the States." He said 'was' as if it had been some time ago.

"How long have you been in Paris?"

"Why?"

"Just wondering." Jesus, talk about blood and stones.

"Two years."

"That long? You must be like a local at this stage."

He didn't answer. The rest of the evening went by in much the same vein. Finally, he got up and said, "I should probably get going."

"Where? I mean, there's no need to rush off."

"Because I've got nowhere to go?"

"Look, you don't have to be so defensive. I'm just trying to help."

"I don't need help." He made for the door. "Thank you for the dinner. It was very nice."

I heard him go down the stairs and open the door. I looked out the window and watched him walk down the street. He didn't sleep in the porch that night.

Or the next night. I wasn't sure what I had done to upset him so much, but whatever it was I didn't want him gone. I couldn't get him out of my mind. I was distracted for days, unable to work, just thinking about him. I was a little obsessed, I suppose.

The next day, I was in my studio and there was a knock at the door. It was him.

"I came to get my clothes. And to apologise. I was rude the other night. I'm not used to … being in people's company. Before the other night, I'd hardly spoken two words to another person in months."

"I understand," I said. "Come in. I'll get your stuff."

He followed me up to the apartment. I made us some coffee. As we sat there in silence, I had this awful feeling that I might not see him again. So, I took my chance.

"Would you model for me?"

"Model?"

"Yeah. For a painting. Or a drawing. Whatever."

"Why me?"

"I don't know. I think you'd make a good study."

"Without clothes?"

"Whatever you're comfortable with."

"What do people normally do?"

"I normally have nude models, male and female. But it's entirely up to you."

"Now?"

"Whenever. We can do it now, if you'd like."

"Okay."

I was surprised he'd agreed so readily. I didn't find out until later the reason why.

"There's a screen there, if you want to get changed."

"No, it's fine," he said. I was surprised. He started to undress in front of me. I had thought his reticence was self-consciousness about his body, but I could see now that it wasn't. He took his clothes off casually and dropped them on the floor. He did it naturally, without thinking. You know the way that some people do? Others are more conscious of it when they undress. Either because they're self-conscious, or because they know exactly the effect it can have.

His body looked exactly as I'd imagined it. Like his arms, the rest of him was all bone and muscle. It was so striking that I found myself staring.

"Is this okay?" he said. "The pose."

"That's great." I went behind the easel and started to sketch. I started talking to try to put him at ease.

"What do you do?" I was surprised I'd never asked him that before. The answer surprised me even more.

"I was a painter." He used the past tense.

"You stopped?"

"Yes. Months ago. That's why this is good. It's good to be in a studio again. Just to smell the oils and the paints."

"If there's any day I'm not here, you want to come in ... "

He just shook his head.

"Why did you stop painting?"

"It's funny, y'know, this image people have of artists as these dark, brooding people, obsessed with pain. I was never like that. You know the idea they have that the artist always pours their pain and heartache into their work. I don't know, maybe it's true for other people. Not for me. I just stopped. I couldn't do it. I couldn't pick up a paintbrush. I just didn't have ... I don't know. Whatever it is that makes someone like you get up in the morning and want to paint. I lost that. Maybe, the pain was just too much. Maybe, it's just not who I am anymore."

"What pain?"

"I was like you two years ago when I came here. Full of life, wanting to change the world with my painting. Wanting to paint every day. I met a girl. She modelled for me. She was beautiful. But, more than beautiful. Everything about her. Of course, later I found out all about her, what she was like. I fell in love with her. But, at first, it was her face and her body. You know what it's like. Like the way you're looking at me. I don't mean that ... well, you know what I mean. You see something, something in the human form. All artists see it. That's why they've painted nudes from the beginning of time." I couldn't believe how much was flowing out of him. Had the painting released all this? He went on. "I was fascinated by her. She became the only one I wanted to paint. Of course, one thing led to another. We talked, I found out who she was, the things she liked, the things she didn't like. What made her laugh, what made her sad. I fell in love with her, hard and heavy."

"I should have known she wasn't made for this world. She was too sensitive. I didn't see it. I saw everything else about her, but I just never saw that. I knew she was fiercely intelligent, I knew she was beautiful, I knew she was kind. So, you would think then that her sensitivity would have been obvious to me? But I thought she was able for anything. I'd fallen into this art scene, one of those underground avant-garde scenes. Idiots, basically. Of course, I couldn't see that at the time. To me, these were the people I'd always wanted to meet when I was living in Minnesota. The kinds of people I would see in the arty movies that came on the TV late at night, or you'd see in the arts section of *The New York Times*."

"I thought she liked the scene too. But she didn't. She liked me and she liked being with me. And I liked being at parties, so she came to the parties. But really, she would have been happier at home with me." He hung his head. "What a fucking idiot. I had this beautiful, wonderful girl who loved me and wanted to spend all her time with me. We could have been in my apartment together every night, being with each other. Instead, I chose to stand with her in a room full of complete strangers who also happened to be complete assholes. I guess what happened is karma. I introduced her to that world, and she was seduced by it. By the drugs. First speed. Then coke. Then heroin. Once that got hold of her, there was no getting her out."

"She moved further and further away from me. That stuff hollowed out all the real parts of her until there was nothing left. A few months into it, she left me. Never said where she was going, who she was going to. Not that it mattered. It wasn't like she'd left me for a person. She left me for the dope."

"I looked for her. I'd go to the clubs we used to go to, the places we used to hang out. I saw some familiar faces but never her. It was like she'd just disappeared. She was a ghost to me. I knew why. I'd seen that drug take people before. Once it gets hold of you, you're no longer that person who goes to parties or hangs out. You're someone who lies on a filthy mattress, in a filthy backroom somewhere, just waiting to score. I knew that's where she was now."

"About a month after that, I heard from a friend of a friend that she was dead. Again, no-one knew for sure where she was, it was just something that was going around on the grapevine. A few weeks after she died, an acquaintance of mine showed up at my door with a photograph. It was of some art opening at this new gallery. She was standing in the background. He told me he'd spotted her straight away and he thought that I'd want to see it."

He showed me the photograph. She looked like a dead rock star. She had that pale washed-out look you see in the photographs from Warhol's Factory. She stood there in just a grubby pair of white knickers, a cigarette in her nicotine-stained fingers, pouting with blood-drained lips.

"I wondered what she was doing there, at this art gallery. Probably hanging around with some other junkie art prick looking to score. I managed to crop her out of the photo and get it blown up.

For the next month, I did nothing but draw that photo of her. I hardly ate or slept. I never left the apartment. I just drew and painted her. My money had long since run out, and I hadn't sold anything in months so I couldn't pay the rent. I was evicted. I don't even know what happened to my stuff. Landlord probably threw it all out. All the paintings of her. I still have the photo though."

"I don't even know where she's buried. I don't know where her grave is to go and say goodbye to her."

At that point, he just stopped talking. It was as though he'd run out of anything else to say. I'd long since stopped drawing him and was just standing there, listening to him. I didn't know what to say either. What do you say to that kind of pain? So, I just drew him. And I continued to draw him, and he continued to come model for me. He had no interest in painting anymore. Whatever light had enabled him to do that had long since gone out. But, the modelling, sitting for me, watching me draw, that seemed to help. I tried to put it down on the canvas, what he was feeling. I thought the combination of talking about it and me putting it down on the canvas might help him.

At that point, I was in love with him. It was ironic how the whole thing played out. Just like he'd said about her. He'd painted her, he'd fallen in love with her, and she'd died. I'd painted him, I'd fallen in love with him, and then he died. Drugs as well. But not the kind that had taken her. Pills. An overdose. I don't know if he wanted to die, or if it was an accident.

I suppose it doesn't matter either way.

A TOWN CALLED WINTER

("Yeah, Oh Yeah" by The Magnetic Fields)

A TOWN CALLED WINTER

I don't know if the following story is true: I heard it from a bartender, and we all know how reliable they are. But he swore that every word of it happened, just like he said.

It was in Colorado – I don't remember the name of the town. It's ten years ago now. It was near-deserted back then, so God-only-knows if it even exists anymore. Towns out there have a habit of just folding up and blowing away.

I was actually headed another couple of hundred miles, but I'd had my days' worth of driving, and decided to check into a motel. After that, I found the town's only bar, and installed myself on a bar stool with a beer and a whiskey chaser in front of me.

The bar was empty, and I asked the bartender if it was always this quiet – to make conversation more than anything else.

"Nowadays, yeah," he said, cryptically. And then, after a dramatic pause: "Usendn't to be, though."

I figured that was my cue. "What happened?" I asked.

"Aw, you wouldn't believe me if I told you."

At the time, I thought it was a figure of speech, but I later realised how close to the truth it was.

"You ever see that movie *The Shining*?" he said. He looked from side to side as he said it, even though the bar was empty.

"Sure."

"Well, that's what it's like up here in the wintertime. In September, it starts to snow; by October, the only way in or out is by snow plough or helicopter." Another dramatic pause. "That'll do funny things to a person's mental state." The way he said 'mental state' made it sound like he had read the words on a pamphlet at the doctor's office.

"It all started in the winter of '88. I was Mayor back then, if you can believe that." He looked around at the empty bar, as though he couldn't believe it himself. "There was this young couple lived in town ... wife was a schoolteacher. Pretty little thing, in a small town kinda way. The husband was a truck driver. They lived next door to this other couple ... woulda been a good ten years older than them, I'd say. But, by all accounts, they were good friends back then. The husbands use to go to ballgames together, and the wives were in the local ladies' sewing circle."

He said it had started out as a joke, as these things usually do. A bit of innocent sexual innuendo. Two guys having a beer at the local bar, start breaking each other's balls, talking about swapping wives. But eventually, it left the bar and moved to the kitchen. The guys started joking with their wives about it. And then, it stopped being a joke. Especially when the wives became curiously interested.

"It was strange, you know? I mean, guys, sure. Guys will do anything for a piece of ass. But women aren't so quick to do that sort of thing. Especially around these parts. At least, that's what I would've thought. Until they all started saying yes."

He said he figured it was a lot to do with the isolation. Men and women stuck together like that for three months, never seeing the outside world, just locked up with their families – that'll do funny things to people. They'll do anything to relieve the boredom.

He said that it started with the two guys and their couple of beers in the bar. And then, plans were made. The subject was never specifically broached by any of them; it was just skirted around, like these things are in small towns. But all four of them knew what was going on. So, one Friday night, Ethel dropped her kids off at Joanie's house for a sleepover. They left all their kids with a sitter and the two women headed back to Ethel's. About an hour later, Larry and Joe arrived home from the bar with a few six-packs, and things went from there.

But there are no secrets in a small town – except for the really bad ones. Everything else always comes out one way or another. Whether it was Larry or Joe bragging, or whether the sitter noticed something when Joe and Ethel came home one night, or whether it was just the good old-fashioned rumour mill, in the end it got out what was happening. Of course, again, it wasn't broached openly; it was just whispered about. But it was the strangest thing, the bartender said, because instead of condemning them, the town – for the most part – wanted to know how to join in.

People were curious; they wanted to know how you went about this kind of thing. Did they pair off, or was it just a free-for-all? How far were you allowed to go? And, most importantly, was anyone else allowed to join in? And so, it started to gather momentum. It moved from the couple's houses to a few houses around that neighbourhood, and then beyond that to other neighbourhoods. Pretty soon, most of the town was at it.

But again, it was never specifically spoken about. Everybody just knew. People would turn up, there'd be a few drinks, maybe a few cocktail sausages, and then everyone would pair off. There were no keys in bowls or anything like that; everyone just implicitly knew who they were to pair off with. And – although it might sound like an orgy – there were never more than two people with each other at a time. It really was what it claimed to be – a partner swap – that's all. The locals may have been liberal enough to swap partners, but they weren't going to engage in any kind of deviant activity like orgies. For a start, there was no way you were going to get two men from that neck of the woods under a blanket together unless they were on a hunting trip.

Of course, it probably would have been better if they *had* all screwed each other; then the jealousy wouldn't have set in.

That's when things started to go awry in this little town in Colorado.

"It's the way of these things, I suppose," the barman said, sounding like a therapist again. "Sex is like everything else in life ... people form alliances, people have favourites. Things aren't always equal. I guess you can't have a whole town fucking each other ... excuse my French ... without expecting something to go wrong. And go wrong it did."

"In what way?"

"Well, people still went to their get-togethers, but now certain people were spending more time with certain other people, and their husbands and wives were getting pissed off. I mean, these people weren't swapping partners anymore ... they were basically having affairs. Naturally, jealousy reared its ugly head. I mean it's one thing to screw random neighbours, it's a whole other thing to screw *specific* neighbours."

"By springtime, the ice was starting to melt but the atmosphere in this town was frosty as hell. There was a tension there. And what made it worse was, now that the roads were cleared, people were starting to come and go again, and things were getting back to normal. All the parties stopped. But not everybody stopped. There were all sorts of illicit liaisons going on all over the town. Some people suspected, some didn't. Some suspected when there was nothing going on. It was crazy. It had to come to a head, and it did. The sheriff shot the postman."

"No shit."

"Yup. Sheriff came home from work early one day and caught the postman and the wife red-handed. According to what she told people afterwards, he didn't stop to think about it for a second, just pulled his gun and popped him right in the head. Killed him outright. Would have done for her too probably but she jumped out the window. Broke her leg in three places, but that's nothing to what could have happened. A neighbour saw her and came over to help her ... that's how she got away with her life."

"I guess it was a wake-up call for the town. We couldn't hide our heads in the sand any longer. People had to own up to each other what was going on, before someone else got hurt. Some people decided to stay together, but they knew they couldn't stay in town here, so most of them moved. Others split up and couldn't stand the sight of each other, so most of them moved too. Pretty soon it was like a ghost town."

"What about you?" I asked.

"Well, my wife left me three years before, so I was single. You're not much use at a wife swap, you don't have a wife. So, I couldn't take part, but I couldn't do anything to stop it either. But I've lived here all my life ... this is my home. Figure I'll stick around for the few years that are left."

With that, the door opened, and an elderly man walked in and took a seat at the bar. The bartender went to serve him, and I finished my whiskey chaser and headed back to my motel.

GHOST ESTATE
("Moonlight Motel" by Bruce Springsteen)

GHOST ESTATE

The affair started – as most things do in Ireland – over drinks. It's how most things end as well, come to that.

You're born, and drinks are poured to "wet the baby's head", and from then on, the rest of your life is counted out – not in years and hours – but in pints and shorts. From communion to 21st birthday, marriage to retirement, and finally, death. Someone is toasting your health before you're born, and they're still there raising a glass to you after you've been put in the ground.

It was supposed to be a night out for the four of us – myself, my wife, Joanne, and Marcus and Sarah – the couple who lived across the street. It was semi-regular occurrence – a catch up that happened every few months, or whenever work and sitters allowed. But that night, Joanne had a stomach bug. I texted Sarah to tell her and she texted back:

Oh no! A perfect storm. Marcus is stuck in work as well. And I really needed a drink tonight.

Normally, I would have suggested that we reschedule, but for some reason I told her if she still wanted to, we could go, just the two of us.

I was halfway through my first pint before I realised we'd never been out alone together before. If it was the four of us, Marcus would usually spend a lot of the night talking about work. He had a high-level job that he seemed to care a lot about; I had a low-level job that I didn't give a shit about. So, it usually ended up with Marcus doing most of the talking about how much stress he was under. Then, after a few pints had been downed, the conversation would inevitably turn to our estate. And – like a bad penny – the question of the petition would raise its head once again.

We had both been one of the first couples to buy on the estate. It was during the final years of the Celtic Tiger. Demand for houses was still sky-high, so we'd both bought from the plans. We moved in after they had built the first fifty houses. They built about another hundred and then the crash happened. The builder ran out of money, the workers downed their tools, and the rest of the estate was left unfinished. Half-built houses and roads, streetlights either never installed or never hooked up.

"It's a fucking disgrace, Dan," Marcus would say. "The council are laughing at us. It's been six years since they stopped building those houses and nothing has been done."

"I know. You're right."

"That's why I think we should really start this petition. Put pressure on the council and get them to knock down those eyesores."

"I just don't see what a couple of hundred signatures is gonna do."

"It could be more than a couple of hundred. It could be a *lot* more. We could go around to all the other housing estates in the area

... we could go into town, set up outside the shopping centre. It could make a difference."

Eventually, I would distract him with some shiny object or half-arsed promise of support, and the notion of the petition would be put to rest again for another few months.

But now that Sarah and I were alone, it was different. There was twenty minutes or so of awkward small talk, but then we got into a groove. There was no talk of work or our estate. Instead, we talked about music and movies. We were both 90s teenagers, so we talked about "Pulp Fiction" and "sex, lies, and videotape", Nirvana and REM. I told her she looked a little like Uma Thurman in "Pulp Fiction" and she blushed. I've never really liked women with short, bobbed haircuts, but her resemblance to Mia Wallace mitigated that. Maybe it was the drinks – or the fact that we were having an interesting conversation – but I noticed things about her that I never had before. Her dark sense of humour. Her infectious laugh. We stayed a little too long and drank a little too much, so by the time the barman was calling time, we realised we had better call a taxi.

We sat in silence in the backseat as the taxi made its way from the city to the suburbs. But it wasn't an uneasy silence – that had been filled with something else. As the taxi pulled off the main road and into the entrance to our estate, I heard Sarah shout, "I need to get out!" The driver hit the brakes, stopping the car right in the middle of the road, and shouted back, "Don't fucking puke in the backseat of my car." Sarah pushed the door open and jumped out, almost falling to the ground. I tossed a twenty at the driver and jumped out after her, pulling her up off the middle of the road and dragging her towards the footpath. As the taxi did a U-turn and pulled back out onto the main road, I looked down at her sitting on the ground at my feet, her head between her knees.

"You okay?" I said.

"I'm fine. I just needed some air." She reached out her hand. "Help me up."

I grabbed her hand and pulled her up – a little too forcefully – because she stumbled and fell against me, starting to laugh. And then we were kissing. It just seemed to happen. I don't even remember thinking about it, although I suppose I must have. And if I hadn't been thinking about it then, I had certainly thought of it before. We stood there, our hands gripping each other's faces, our tongues searching each other out, before either of us realised where we were. When we stopped for a moment, I said, "Sarah, someone's gonna see us out here."

"Come on," she said. She started to half-walk, half-run towards one of the abandoned houses on the outskirts of the estate.

We walked quietly through waist-high weeds and bracken. Even in the dark – by only the moonlight – I could see the dereliction of the abandoned houses: gardens that nature had reclaimed, some windows boarded up, others left broken. I followed her around the side of one of the houses. There was a sliding patio, the glass having long since been smashed. We made our way carefully inside, the sound of glass and other detritus crunching beneath our feet. As soon as we were inside, Sarah grabbed me and kissed me again. But this time, I'd sobered up a little.

"I don't know ... should we ..."

She stared into my eyes. "I know," she said.

I wasn't sure what that meant. But she continued kissing me. It was surreal as I stood there, kissing her, the only sounds the night insects and the glass beneath our feet. After a minute, she stopped, took me by the hand and started to lead me upstairs.

"Where are you going?"

She didn't answer, just kept walking, holding my hand. When we got to the landing, she took out her phone and turned the flashlight on, leading me into one of the bedrooms. There was a mattress on the floor. It was filthy, but she didn't even stop to think about it. She pulled me down and started kissing me again. At this point, I'd stopped caring.

She pulled down my jeans and underwear and took me in her hand. I slid my hand up her skirt and felt my fingers go inside her.

"I don't have protection ..." I heard myself say, clumsily.

"It's okay."

She lifted up her skirt, pulled her underwear to one side, and guided me inside her. When I came, I pulled out and put my fingers in again until she came too. We lay there, spent. Almost immediately, the thoughts started.

"Are you sure it was okay?" I said.

"It was great."

"No ... I mean ... without protection."

"I'm on the pill."

"Yeah, but still ..."

She pushed me off her gently, adjusted her underwear, and pulled down her skirt. "Jesus, you know how to ruin a moment."

"Sorry. I didn't mean to."

"It's fine," she said, getting up. "I have to go."

"I'll walk with you."

We walked in silence to her house. The light was still on in their bedroom. She went inside without a word.

It was two weeks before I heard from her again. I was in work and got a text.

Can you meet me tonight? 8pm, the same place.

I stared at the text, panic rising up inside me. I wondered if something had happened – was there something she needed to tell me? All the different scenarios played out in my brain for the rest of the day in work, and over dinner. My stomach was in ribbons by the time I finally got to the deserted house at eight. She was in the same room, standing with her back to me looking out the window. She turned around when I walked in.

"Is everything all right?" I said.

"Yeah. I just wanted to see you."

I felt the tension leave my body. She walked over and started to kiss me. I know I should have stopped her then. I'd spent a day having a nervous breakdown about what might have happened and now I'd just gotten a reprieve. And, just like that, I was about to put myself back in the same position again. It was beyond stupid. But none of that really went through my mind as I stood there that night, not until the next day. Very little went though my mind as I stood there tasting the sharp tang of her lipstick, my hand running up beneath her top and feeling her breasts.

She reached into her bag and took out a sheet.

"I brought this," she said. She tossed it onto the mattress and put her hand into her bag again, pulling out a box of condoms. "And these."

The weeks that followed were a kind of madness. Some kind of disassociation from real life while still carrying out the daily routines that real life necessitated. I've wondered since if that's what people with dissociative mental illness feel like – almost like existing in two separate worlds simultaneously.

One night, we were lying on the filthy mattress – the smell of sweat and sex mixing with the stench of mould – when she said: "Do you love Joanne?"

"What kind of question is that? If I loved her, I'd hardly be here, would I?" Even as I said it, I could hear the defensiveness in my voice.

"Why not? You can love someone and still want to do this. I love Marcus."

"You say that …"

"No, I do. I know how I feel."

"But if you love someone … I mean *really* love someone … isn't that supposed to be enough?"

She leaned on her elbow and looked at me. "Enough for what?"

"To make you happy."

"I am happy."

"Okay. Enough to make you content. I mean, if you love someone aren't they supposed to be enough for you? To not want to go elsewhere … to do something like this?"

She got up from the mattress and wrapped her cardigan around her naked frame. "Do you remember years ago … Mick Jagger, the singer with the Rolling Stones … he was married to a supermodel …"

"Jerry Hall."

She walked over to the window and stood with her back to me, looking out. "Yeah. And he cheated on her."

"He cheated on her a *lot*."

"Well, this was when they finally split up. I remember reading an article … it was written by a guy, of course … and he was saying how people were shocked that Jagger would leave this beautiful supermodel to have an affair with somebody. Everyone was saying, 'Why would you go out for hamburger when you can have steak at home?'" She turned her head slightly and looked over at me. "And the guy writing the article said, 'Because sometimes, you don't want steak. Sometimes you just want a hamburger.'"

"That sounds like someone trying to rationalise having an affair."

"Who said I need to rationalise it?"

I hadn't meant her; I meant the other guy. But the way she said it stopped me in my tracks. She'd made her point.

We never talked about life outside those four walls. Our jobs or people we knew, or anything like that. We just talked about music and movies mostly.

She asked me one night how I listened to music.

"I've still got my old CDs," I told her. "But to be honest, nowadays Spotify is just handier."

"I hate Spotify. I still listen to my old records. Everything is so commodified nowadays. Safe and boring. Listening to vinyl reminds me of a time when life was unpredictable … when anything could happen. You know what I mean?"

I didn't at the time, but I think I do now.

It had been about three weeks since I'd seen Sarah, when Joanne called to me from downstairs one day.

"Dan … look out the front window."

Across the street, movers were emptying the contents of Marcus and Sarah's house and putting them into a truck. They seemed to be working under their own guidance. There was no sign of either Marcus or Sarah. I heard Joanne come into the room behind me.

"Did they say anything to you?" she said. There was something like hurt in her voice.

"No."

"That's odd." She peered out through the blinds. "Should we go over there? Say goodbye?"

"No point. I think they're gone."

    I left the house without a coat or any idea where I was going. I just needed to get out. Too many thoughts were spinning around in my head, I couldn't pin any one down. Five minutes later, I stopped, looked up, and realised I was standing outside the abandoned house.

    I went upstairs to the bedroom and stood at the window, as she'd done many times. I stood there wondering what she'd been looking at, what she'd been thinking. After about half an hour, I finally left the house, took one last look at it, and headed back towards my house. On the way back, I stopped at the first occupied house I came to and knocked at the door. The man who answered gave me a look of recognition and curiosity.

    "Hi," I said. "I'm living in number 12. I wanted to talk to you about starting a petition to get the derelict houses demolished. We need to knock down those eyesores."

TO THE READER

Firstly, thank you so much for buying *The Highway Kind*. I hope you enjoyed it.

As an independent author, reviews and word of mouth are my lifeblood, and help bring my books to the attention of other readers.

If you liked this book, I would be so grateful if you could take five minutes to leave a review (doesn't matter how short) on Amazon. (Just search for "Derek Flynn, The Highway Kind")

Thanks so much, and I hope to see you back here in the future.

ABOUT THE AUTHOR

Derek Flynn is a writer, actor, and musician based in Waterford, Ireland. He is co-founder of the Theatre Vamps theatre group, and co-founder and co-editor of the literary journal, *The Waxed Lemon*. He can be found online at: https://www.derekflynnbooks.com/

ALSO BY DEREK FLYNN

Broken Falls

Wyoming cop, John Ryan, receives a package of letters from a recently deceased priest addressed to John's late father, begging for his forgiveness for something the priest had done.

Unravelling the story behind the letters leads John to the remote fishing village of Broken Falls, Newfoundland, a place filled with strange and colourful characters, whose secrets are as old as the village itself. As he attempts to find out what it was the dead priest did – and how he died – John must confront his own past and the secrets that his father tried so hard to hide.

The Dead Girls

(Voted one of the BEST BOOKS OF 2019 **by the ROSBC – Ireland's biggest online book club)**

When ex-cop turned private detective, John Ryan, is hired to find a missing girl, he makes a horrifying discovery: a trail of young women brutally murdered, their bodies dumped on the side of the highways of America.

A young girl running away from home is haunted by images of a missing girl. Neither she nor John realise how their paths will cross when they come into contact with one man. A man who searches the highways for victims. A sadistic killer known only as The Trucker.

The Dark

John Ryan has had his share of strange cases. But none as strange as the man who turns up claiming he can't remember who he is. As John attempts to find out the mystery man's identity, the lights suddenly go out in Choketown.

And then the murders start. The Choketown Killer has returned. And John's client becomes the number one suspect. With his city in the grip of a blackout, John begins the hunt for the serial killer as the body count rises and the city teeters on the brink of spiralling out of control. But the question is: who can he trust?

The Bone Lake – A Short Novel

Jimmy Durand has spent half his life on the wrong side of a law. Now in his middle age – working odd jobs in the wealthy town of Lakeside – Jimmy figures that's all behind him.

But he's wrong.

When a phone call for a routine job turns into something much more sinister, Jimmy finds himself embroiled in a murder case. Falling back on his old skills, he takes matters into his own hands and soon realises that somewhere in Lakeside – in the trailer parks or the gilded mansions, or even in the police department – someone is trying to frame him from murder.

Black Wood – A standalone thriller

"How far would you go to get out?" This is the question three unlikely friends living in a dead-end town in America ask each other. The answer would come to haunt them.

The narrator is a writer in his late 30s, making a living as a college lecturer. Samantha Pierce, a woman he hasn't seen in twenty years, re-enters his life and tells him she is being blackmailed – because of something they did years before in the Black Wood. As they try to identify their blackmailer, the narrator recalls the events of the summer they graduated High School – the summer that led to the fateful night in the Black Wood when their question was answered, and they did something that changed their lives forever.

The Ballad of New York

(Voted one of the BEST READS OF 2021 **by Waterford Libraries)**

"I lived in a rented house with a rented companion, both of us living rented lives."

Stuck in a broken relationship and a dead-end job, a young man leaves Ireland and heads to New York to try to make it as a musician. What follows is at once a story about growing up in Ireland in the late 80s and 90s; a love letter to New York; and a testament to the power of music and the songs we carry with us throughout our lives.

Printed in Great Britain
by Amazon

Reviews for Derek Flynn's other novels

Broken Falls

"Flynn's debut [has] a cast of strong relatable characters with all the ingredients of a perfect crime drama that is gritty, riveting and so real that you can taste it."

- Adele O' Neill, author of *Behind a Closed Door*

The Dead Girls

"If you are not following the private detective John Ryan series, then go start. You will love it ... a cracker of a book and a blinding series."

- Book Reviews For U

The Dark

"Grabs the reader from the opening page."

- Louise Phillips, bestselling crime author

Black Wood

"An addictive, fresh, clever thriller ..."

- Behind Green Eyes Book Reviews

The Ballad of New York

"Confessional, unapologetic, and fiercely engaging ... essential reading."

- *Waterford News and Star*